for Nan and Grandad

HODDER CHILDREN'S BOOKS

First published in Great Britain in 2017 by Hodder and Stoughton

Text and illustrations copyright © Ellie Sandall 2017

A CIP catalogue record of this book
is available from the British Library.

HB ISBN: 978 1 444 93383 3
PB ISBN: 978 1 444 93384 0

10 9 8 7 6 5 4 3 2 1

Printed and bound in China

Hodder Children's Books
An imprint of
Hachette Children's Group
Part of Hodder and Stoughton
Carmelite House
50 Victoria Embankment
London EC4Y 0DZ

An Hachette UK Company
www.hachette.co.uk

www.hachettechildrens.co.uk

Ellie ☆ Sandall

EVERYBUNNY
Count!

4...

5...   6...   7...

Hodder Children's Books

Fox and bunnies like to play,
all together, every day.

Playing **hide-and-seek** today...

Take your places, everyone.
Ready or not, here we come!

The search for fox has just begun.
Everybunny count to ONE!

We found some birds, away they flew.
Everybunny count to **TWO!**

We've spotted something in the tree.
Everybunny count to THREE!

Tiny creatures in my paw.
Everybunny count to FOUR!

Check the water, in we dive.
Everybunny count to FIVE!

Look who's hiding in the sticks.
Everybunny count to SIX!

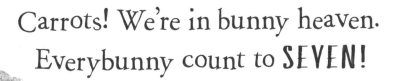

Carrots! We're in bunny heaven.
Everybunny count to SEVEN!

Where's that fox? It's getting late.
Everybunny count to EIGHT!

Sleepy bunnies in a line.

Everybunny count to **NINE!**

Through a bush, behind some rocks.

Everybunny look...

Now take a peek inside the den.

EVERYBUNNY
COUNT...

Foxes, bunnies,

one to ten.

Let's play **hide-and-seek** again!